It's Time

By
Judith Mammay

Illustrated by
Todd Fargo

Jason & Nordic Publishers
Hollidaysburg, Pennsylvania

Note for parents and teachers:
In sharing this book with children, you may wish to explain that the mouse included at the edge of each illustration shows us what Tommy is feeling. It helps to understand feelings that Tommy has trouble expressing.

It's Time
Text and Illustrations copyright© 2007 Jason & Nordic Publishers

Library of Congress Cataloging-in-Publication Data

Library of Congress Cataloging-in-Publication Data

Mammay, Judith, 1943-
  It's time / by Judith Mammay ; illustrated by Todd Fargo.
      p. cm.
  Summary: Because Tommy has autism he likes routine, and when the unexpected happens, he must try hard to use words instead of having a tantrum.
  ISBN-10: 0-944727-20-4 (paper bdg. : alk. paper)
  ISBN-13: 978-0-944727-20-1 (paper bdg. : alk. paper)
  ISBN-10: 0-944727-21-2 (lib. bdg. : alk. paper)
  ISBN-13: 978-0-944727-21-8 (lib. bdg. : alk. paper)
  [1. Autism--Fiction. 2. Schools--Fiction.] I. Fargo, Todd, 1963- ill. II. Title. III. Title: It is time.
  PZ7.M3119Its 2007
  [E]--dc22
                        2006039425

Paper edition EAN 978-0944727-20-1
Library edition EAN 978-0-944727-21-8

Printed in the U.S.A.
On acid free paper

Dedicated to

Matthew

and

to all children
with or without autism
who work hard to remember
to "use their words"

Tommy sat on the floor of his bedroom and picked up a red brick. He placed it on the wall he was building. His mother walked into the room. Tommy didn't look up.

"I'm building a garage," Tommy said. "I will park seven cars in the garage."

"That's a nice one," Mom said. She smiled. "But you'll have to finish it later. It's time for school."

"NO! I'm making a garage," Tommy yelled.

"It's time for school," Mom repeated. "Your bus will be here in ten minutes."

Tommy swung his arm and knocked the garage down. Then he threw himself on the floor and screamed. He kicked his feet and pounded the floor with his fists.

"Use your words," Mom said. She bent down and rubbed Tommy's back.

"I can't!" Tommy screamed again.

He took a deep breath and tried to calm down. It was hard to stop building when he wasn't finished.

Mom stood up and said, "Two minutes, then it will be time to watch for the bus."

Tommy took another deep breath and stood up. "Time for school."

Tommy rubbed his eyes. "First I pick up blocks. Then I get on bus."

"Good job," Mom said and gave him a hug.

Tommy picked up his blocks and went outside to wait for the bus with his mother.

At school, Tommy put his backpack in his cubby and hung up his jacket.

His friend Jake ran through the door and dropped his backpack on the floor.

"Hi, Tommy. Let's play a game," said Jake. He smiled and put his arm around Tommy's shoulder.

Tommy pulled away from Jake. He didn't like it when people touched him or got too close. Sometimes it made his heart pound fast. Sometimes he wanted to run away, but he had learned that was not safe.

Sometimes Tommy forgot to say "hi."

"It's time to do morning work," Tommy said. He liked to help Jake follow the classroom rules.

"First, put away backpacks and hang up jackets. Then do morning work." It was the same every day. He liked everything to be in order.

Tommy waited for Jake to take care of his backpack and jacket.

At their seats Tommy looked at the paper on his desk.

Jake reached into his pocket and took out a small car.

"Zoom, zoom," said Jake. He raced the car around his paper while other children were still putting away their backpacks and greeting their friends.

"Time to work," Tommy said. He took out his pencil and wrote on his paper. He tried to stay calm, but it was hard when Jake and the other children were making so much noise.

He looked around and started breathing faster. Then he put his pencil down, covered his ears, and yelled, "TOO LOUD!"

All the children stopped and looked at Tommy.

Mrs. Brown walked over to Tommy. "It's okay, Tommy," she said and put her hand on his shoulder. "Boys and girls, please use your inside voices. Remember, when it is a little noisy, it sounds like everyone is screaming to Tommy, because of his autism. We can help him by working quietly."

Jake looked at Tommy. "You're no fun!" he grumbled, but he put his car away and took out his pencil.

Mrs. Brown walked by and looked at the boys' papers.

"Good work, Jake," she said. "Good job, Tommy. Circle time in five minutes."

Tommy worked for three more minutes and then put his paper in his desk.

"All done," he said. Tommy liked it when Mrs. Brown gave him a five-minute warning. He had learned that it helped him keep calm and gave him time to finish what he was doing.

After circle, Tommy did his reading. When his work was too hard, he remembered to raise his hand and use his words.

"I need help," he said. He didn't scream or throw his work on the floor like he sometimes did in first grade. And Tommy always said "time to work" when he saw Jake looking around or playing.

After reading it was time for math. Tommy liked math. He was good at math. He could already multiply like the third graders. His classmates thought he was very smart.

At the end of the day, Mrs. Brown said, "Please put away all work and story books. It's time to go home."

"First clean desk and get homework," Tommy said to himself. "Then get backpack and jacket. Then line up at door for bus." Saying the steps in order helped Tommy to understand and remember what to do.

The classroom phone rang and Mrs. Brown answered it. When she hung up, she walked toward Tommy.

"Tommy, your mother wants you to wait here for her. She'll pick you up today."

Tommy made his hands into fists. He didn't like changes. He threw himself on the floor.

"Time for bus!" he screeched. "I go on bus!" Tommy kicked his feet. He pounded his fists on the floor. The children near him moved away.

"Tommy, your mother will be here soon," Mrs. Brown said. "Please stop."

She looked at the rest of the class. Some children had their hands over their ears. One girl was crying. "It's okay, boys and girls. Remember it is Tommy's autism that makes him do this. He'll calm down."

"Bus!" yelled Tommy. "Time for bus!"

Jake moved toward Tommy.

"Please don't yell," Jake said. "When you scream, it scares me."

Tommy looked around at his friends. They looked away. "Bus," said Tommy, but he didn't yell.

Jake said, "Maybe you can go on the bus tomorrow."

"Maybe bus tomorrow," Tommy said. He stood up to wait for his mother.

The next day at school Tommy put his backpack and jacket away. He did his morning work and went to circle. Next he did his reading, just like always.

Tommy looked at the clock. "Time for math," he whispered. He waited, but Mrs. Brown didn't say it.

"Boys and girls," said Mrs. Brown. "Today we'll skip math. I have a surprise for you."

Tommy made his hands into fists. His heart began to beat faster. He didn't like surprises. He liked to know what would happen next.

He started to scream and throw himself on the floor, but he stopped. He didn't want to scare the other children. He grabbed both sides of his chair so he would stay in it. "Use words," he whispered to himself.

Tommy called out, "What will happen?"

"Today we're going to see a puppet show by The Kids on the Block!" Mrs. Brown said.

Tommy liked puppets, but it was time for math.

"Then what will happen?" he asked, still holding on to his chair.

"After the puppet show, it'll be lunch time," said Mrs. Brown. "Then we'll do our afternoon activities."

"First puppets, then lunch, then story and science," said Tommy.

"Right," said Mrs. Brown. "Good job using your words."

Tommy smiled. "I like puppets," he said.

Tommy sat between Jake and Mrs. Brown and waited for the puppet show. Tommy held his headphones on his lap.

"Too loud," Tommy whispered when the music started. He put on his headphones and smiled. "Now I like the music."

"Look, the puppet show is starting," Jake said.

Tommy clapped and laughed as the puppets played.

"They're going to fight!" Jake bounced in his seat and laughed.

"NO! No fighting!" said Tommy. "I don't like fighting."

"It's okay," Mrs. Brown said. "See? They're using words to solve their problem so they don't have to fight."

"They can use their words, too." Tommy whispered.

After that, whenever there was a change, Tommy did better using his words.
He always asked, "Then what will happen?" The words helped him know what it was time to do. That helped him stay calm.